BALLOONS

BALLOONS

and Other Poems

Deborah Chandra

Pictures by Leslie Bowman

A Sunburst Book

Farrar Straus Giroux

Library of Congress catalog card number: 89-46144
Published in Canada by HarperCollins*CanadaLtd*
Printed in the United States of America
First edition, 1990
Sunburst edition, 1993

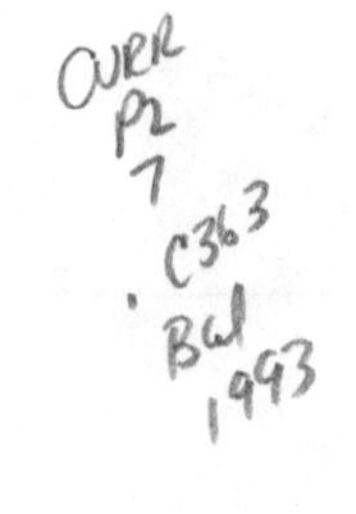

To Pravein with love
D.C.

To K.K.R. with love
L.B.

Contents

BALLOONS

Balloons

Such swollen creatures,
Holding their breath
While they swim
Dreamily from
Room to room.

Swaying slightly,
They wander the air-wisps,
Bumping and rubbing along the walls
Until they feel their fat backs
Bob against the ceiling.

Wanting nothing,
They drift and sleep—
Bald as babies,
Smooth moons of blue and red,
Nodding drowsy, spellbound heads.

Fireworks

A hiss,
Howl,
Rush,
A thunderous roar!
Wild beasts burst
In fiery hordes
To mix with shadows
In the sky,
Flashing teeth
And tiger eyes.

Sizzling tongues,
Leopard spots,
Lion mouths
Red, round, and hot!
Bristling paws
Climb the night,
Golden glowing
Balls of light
That pounce, then sprawl,
There . . .
now there,
and there,
Burning, trembling
In the air—
To fade,
Falling
On earth below;
Soft as milkweed,
Silent as snow.

My Christmas Present

My Christmas present stares at me,
A silver bulge beneath the tree,
Tied with bright red bows.

I pick it up—its ribbons slip
And tingle on my fingertips.
"What can you be?" I whisper low.

I shake and poke and peer at it,
Then put it back and sigh a bit.
It will not tell me what it knows.

Stiffly dressed in shiny clothes
Of silver, waiting silently,
My present sits . . . and stares at me.

Tent

My skin is like
A canvas tent
That's stretched
From bone to bone;
It's cut to measure
Just for me,
I wonder where
It's sewn?
And why can't I
Unzip the front
And roam outside,
Then in?
But here I stay
Each night, each day,
Alone,
Within my skin.

Skeleton

Brittle
As dry grass,
Moonwhite,
Thin;
A clatter
Of cold bones,
No hair,
Heart,
Or skin.
Stepping out
Of black shadows,
He knocks on doors,
Peeks in—
On Halloween,
Remembering
The round warm
World of men.

At the Florist

In an icy chamber
A woman bends over
Cuttings of cold roses,
Their mouths frozen closed.

Sold by the stem:
They stare,
Leaning stiffly,
Blank as stones.

She picks a pink one,
Her warm breath blows
On its pale lips;
And they quiver in a
Soft cough.

Mama's Song

Mama hums a sea-song with her eyes,
A deep blue rising sea-song,
    moving as her eyes move,
    weaving foam across my face.

White gulls whirl overhead,
The sun washes back and forth,
    and I am rocking . . .
            rocking . . .
                like a boat
            in the waves
                of her song.

Piggyback Dad

I don't want the ride to end,
I hug your back.
We ride again
Around the table
Past the chair
Through the kitchen
Up the stairs.
I laugh until I cannot see,
I laugh because you're galloping
As if we are a horse and rider
(We ride crazy-wild together!),
And soon it isn't you and me,
But only one horse—
That is *we*.
Closer than closest we are then,
I hold you tight
Right to the end.

Calling Me

The orange fish
In the pond outside
All stare at
Me
And open wide
Their hollow mouths
For me to see,
As if they're
Calling . . .
          calling me.

I stop.
And listen
Close and still,
To hear
What they keep
Trying to tell
Me, but their
Wet words
Seem to glide
Beneath the lily pads
And hide.
I watch them call,
Their lips grown round;
It's strange—
I never hear
A sound.

Suspense

Wide-eyed
the sunflowers
stare and catch their summer
breath, while I pause, holding basket
and shears.

The Purr

My cat churns
A purple purr—
A throatful
Of pebbles
Turning slowly
Underwater,
Her old song
Bubbles.

Swirling easy
Through the lazy current
Swims a warm mouse-flavored
"Meow."

Autumn Leaves

With shivers and rustles,
Wind-ruffled leaves
Scuttle down gutters,
Wander the sidewalks,
Tumble on brown lawns,
Bunch under trees.
Grieving for summer
With gasps and sighs,
Crackling
And crunching,
They call their
Goodbyes!

Stray Dog

Earth-born beast,
Brown with dust,
Bramblebush and itchweed brushed.

Fur like dry grass,
Wild and thick;
With tongue, lips, jaw you sniff and lick

A language made of
Soft warm smells,
Sticky with thistle sap, that tell

Of far fields
Ripening in the wind;
Whispering, they beckon, bend.

I watch you
Restlessly taste air,
In tightened silence you tremble, stare—

To dance, then
Vanish suddenly,
And something rustles deep in me.

Sun and I

Sun washes down
The morning sky,
And hangs it up
To drip,
Then dry its
Golden light
That
    dribbles
            down
Into puddles
On the ground.
I splatter-splash
Those puddles bright,
And drenched
From head to toe
In light,
I drag out shadows
One by one,
To dip
And wash them
In the sun.

Ribbons of Wind

Clear
ribbons
of
wind
ripple
and swish,
can you
hear them
curl and
twist
among the
leaves?
Great rolls
of windfall
ribbons
rub a
silken
hiss
as they
slip
between
the bushes,
through
the
trees.

Sky

A huge eye—
Blue and moving,
The sky
Opens wide,
Silently
Surrounding me
With its
Gaze.

Fog

An old cold-blooded creature,
Slow and tired, glides—
Out of the ocean's twilight deeps,
Up from the endless tides—
And slides its thick wet belly
Over rocks and sand,
Then turns and rolls upon its back
To scratch against the land.
The fog seeps in and presses
On trees and rocks and mud;
This old cold-blooded creature
Who wants its wet back rubbed.

Burglar

Rain
Creeps
Upon my rooftop
Like a burglar
In the night,
Runs fingers
Round my windows,
Finding everything
Shut tight.
Startled
When the morning dawns,
It dangles from the eaves,
Drops d
o
w
n,
Sneaking away
Without a sound,
Leaving small
Footprints
on
the
Ground.

Snowfall

The leaves are gone,
The world is old,
I hear a whisper from the sky—
The dark is long,
The ground's grown cold,
I hear the snow's white lullaby.

She breathes it softly
Through the air,
While with her gown of flakes she sweeps
The sky, the trees, the ground grown cold,
Singing hush,
        Now hush,
            Now hush,
                Hush,
                  Sleep.

Stars

I liked the way they looked down from the sky
And didn't seem to mind the way I cried.

And didn't say, "Now wipe away those tears,"
Or, "Tell us, tell us what's the matter here!"

But shining through the dark they calmly stayed,
And gently held me in their quiet way.

I felt them watching over me, each one—
And let me cry and cry till I was done.

Night

Silently
The night
Surrounds me,
Folds its soft
Dark arms
Around me;
Weaving shadows,
It whispers low
How it will
Circle, gather,
Grow and make itself
A cradle deep
To hold me closely
While I sleep.

FRANKLIN PIERCE COLLEGE LIBRARY
00082228